Dedicated to

OMRI, WILLA, & JULIA

and

CHRISTOPHER COLWELL
BRAD COMER
ROBERT GUNTRIP
TOMOYUKI-BRYAN-WATANABE

JOHN JEREMY COLTON

WRITTEN BY BRYAN JEFFERY LEECH AND DESIGNED & ILLUSTRATED BY BYRON GLASER & SANDRA HIGASHI

HYPERION BOOKS FOR CHILDREN · NEW YORK

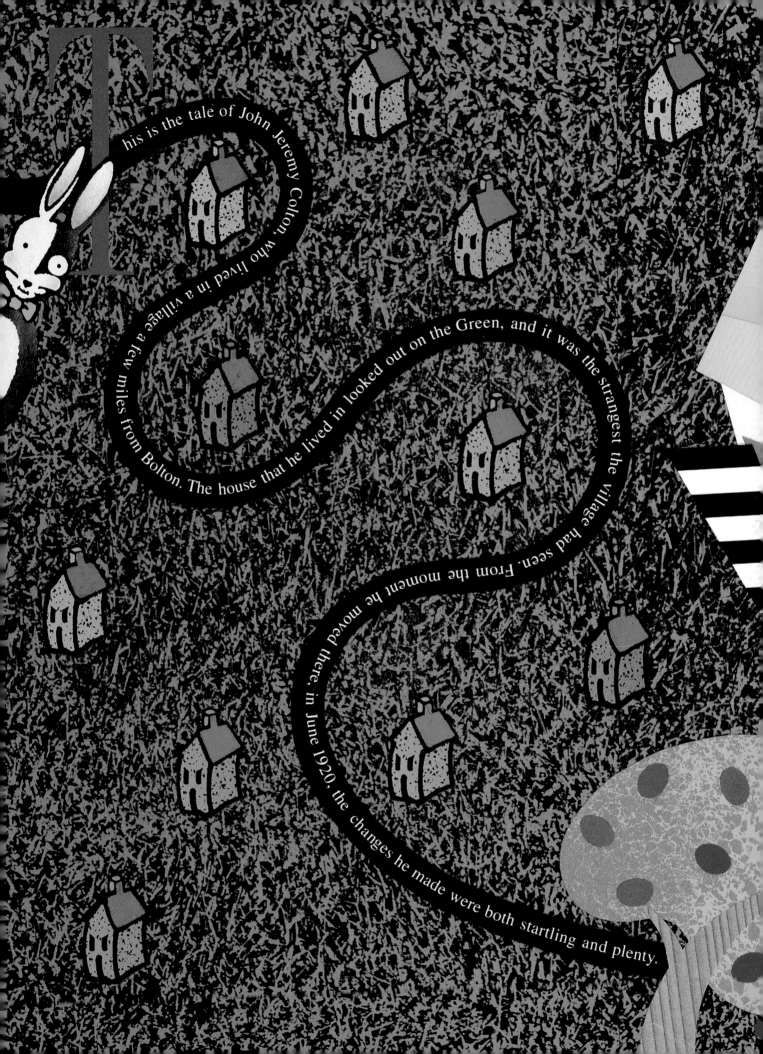

This is the tale of John Jeremy Colton, who lived in a village a few miles from Bolton. The house that he lived in looked out on the Green, and it was the strangest the village had seen. From the moment he moved there, in June 1920, the changes he made were both startling and plenty.

...caused quite a to-do. For the townsfolk who lived there, each man and each woman, considered his taste to be almost

candy-striped shutters

His windows were red and his door a bright blue. His

lime Jell-O.

was the hue of

He painted the walls a buttercup yellow, and the thatch on his roof

INHUMAN. EACH DAY THEY WOULD STARE FROM

CLUCKING AND TUTTING AT HOME

WISHED THAT THEIR NEIGHBOR WOULD MOVE. "SURELY HE

THEIR GRAY CHEERLESS   HOUSES,

WITH THEIR   SPOUSES. FOR EVERYONE

KNOWS THAT WE ALL DISAPPROVE."

John Jeremy Colton, if he were

AWARE, seemed not to WORRY

or BOTHER or care. He whistled and

sang as he strolled down the street,

greeting each person he happened to meet.

But faces were turned. Umbrellas were  lowered.

No one  replied and everyone glowered. "He'll not

win me with smiles!"  sniffed Mrs. Hythe-Potter.

"The man is a bounder, a rogue, and a rotter." The

children  were warned not to go near his gate.

They were led to expect a most terrible fate. But

the more they were told they were not to greet him, the

greater their longing to go there and meet him.

ONE DAY, ON THE GREEN, THEY WERE PLAYING AT CRICKET

WHEN A BOY HIT A BALL WHILE DEFENDING

IT FLEW THROUGH THE AIR LIKE A STAR

THE BREAKING OF GLASS MADE A

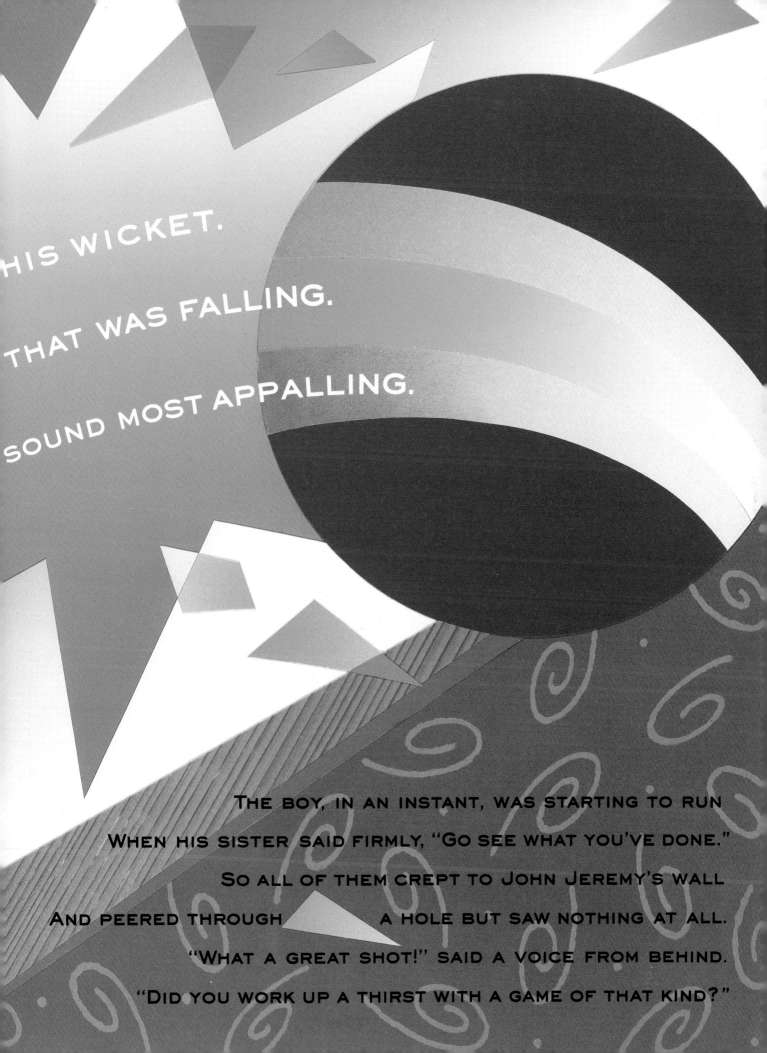

HIS WICKET.

THAT WAS FALLING.

SOUND MOST APPALLING.

THE BOY, IN AN INSTANT, WAS STARTING TO RUN
WHEN HIS SISTER SAID FIRMLY, "GO SEE WHAT YOU'VE DONE."
SO ALL OF THEM CREPT TO JOHN JEREMY'S WALL
AND PEERED THROUGH A HOLE BUT SAW NOTHING AT ALL.
"WHAT A GREAT SHOT!" SAID A VOICE FROM BEHIND.
"DID YOU WORK UP A THIRST WITH A GAME OF THAT KIND?"

JoHn JeRemy caLLed
to the CoOk and the MaiD.
And sOoN tHey reTuRned,
serving **BLUE** LeMoNaDE,

a CaRouSeL CaKe
with CaNdY-CaNe PoLeS and
PiES shaped like *Slippers*
with LiCORiCe SoLeS.

THeRe were SaNDwicHes toO,
shap*ed* *like* BiRds and like FiSheS.
It was StRaNgE FoOd INDEED!
(ThOugh iT TaSted DE*licious*.)

John Jeremy joked

and he told them a riddle.

They sang several songs

while he played the fiddle.

He showed them the treasures

he'd found in strange lands

and his tame hedgehog

that danced on his hands.

The house started shaking with sounds of their fun. It was birthdays and Christmas all rolled into one.

They left when the cuckoo clock called out, "It's four."

"Can we come again, soon?" they asked at the door.

day and week followed week, the house and its owner began to look bleak.

"The man is quite mad!" The children protested, defending their friend. The parents said firmly, "This friendship must end," John

Jeremy thought, when no children came, I said something wrong. I must be to blame. As day followed

They ran home to tell of the good time they'd had, but their parents insisted,

John Jeremy's house was put up for sale. The buttercup walls

seemed suddenly pale. The thatch on the roof was in need of

repair. It looked like a   spider   with   too   little

hair. The children grew sullen. The weather turned gray. The birds

stopped their singing. All joy went away. Still, Mrs. Hythe-Potter

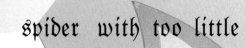

refused to be kind. "I want the man gone—out of sight, out of mind."

Then, one windy night around quarter to three, John Jeremy woke and he happened to see a column of smoke that was starting to pour from a house near the Green, number 74.

"FIRE!

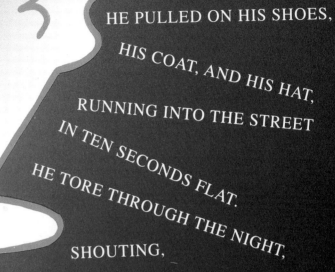

HE PULLED ON HIS SHOES,

HIS COAT, AND HIS HAT,

RUNNING INTO THE STREET

IN TEN SECONDS FLAT.

HE TORE THROUGH THE NIGHT,

SHOUTING,

FIRE! FIRE! FIRE!"

AS THE SMOKE BEGAN BILLOWING

HIGHER AND HIGHER.

HE SHOUTED INSTRUCTIONS:

"RING THE BELL IN THE STEEPLE!"

SOON THE STREETS AND THE GREEN

BEGAN FILLING WITH PEOPLE.

"GET YOUR BUCKETS AND PAILS,"

HE TOLD MR. McGRUMP.

"FORM A LINE DOWN THE STREET

FROM THE HOUSE TO THE PUMP."

He broke down the door

and saw the hall was alight.

At the top of the stairs,

standing frozen with fright,

was a figure he knew

to be Mrs. Hythe-Potter,

the same one who'd called him

"a rogue and a rotter."

"Stay where you are!"

John Jeremy cried.

"I'll climb to the roof.

I'll get you outside!

Someone, give me an axe.

Someone, get me a rope!"

Everyone watched,

but with dwindling hope.

At the side of the house

stood a fragile old tree.

Its uppermost branches

just happened to be

a foot or two higher

than the edge of the roof.

But would the tree hold him?

Of that, he'd no proof.

The tree started creaking.

A branch fell away.

Everyone gasped as they

watched in dismay.

With a push and a leap

he flew through the air.

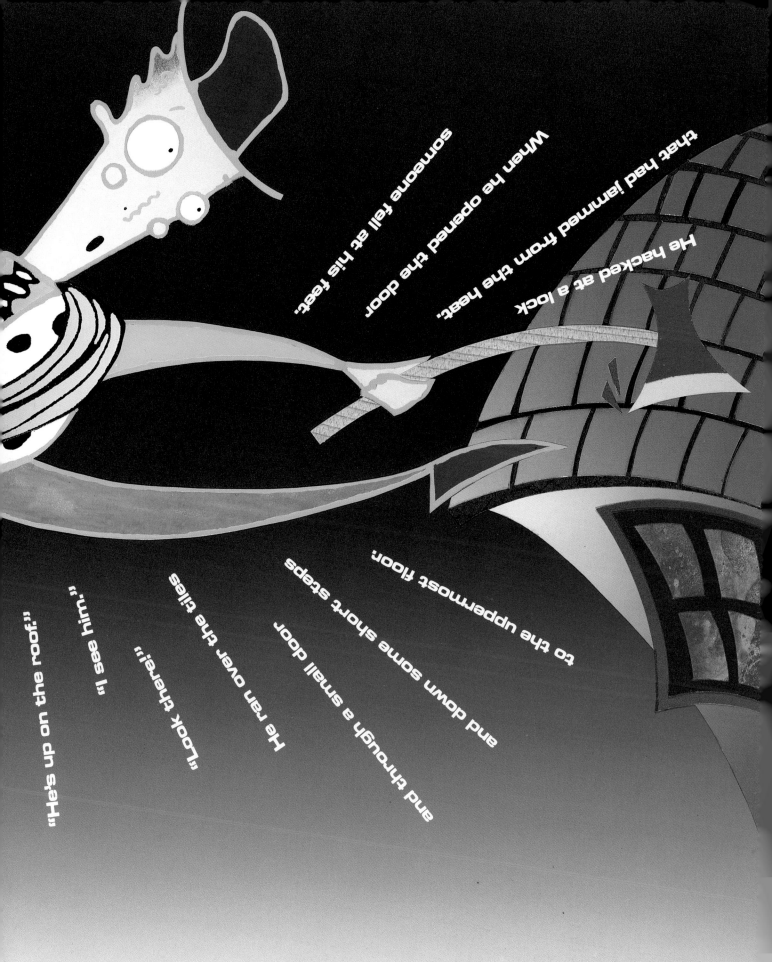

"He's up on the roof!"

"I see him."

"Look there!"

He ran over the tiles

and through a small door

and down some short steps

to the uppermost floor.

When he opened the door

someone fell at his feet.

that had jammed from the heat.

He hacked at a lock

THE COOK AND THE NANNY,
THE BUTLER, THE MAID
ALL LOOKED LIKE THEY'D NEVER
BEEN QUITE SO AFRAID.

IT WAS MRS. HYTHE-POTTER,
HER FACE BLACK WITH DIRT,
BEHIND HER, HER CHILDREN.
AND NO ONE WAS HURT!

SO MRS. HYTHE-POTTER,
NO LONGER ALOOF,
CLAMBERED UP THE SHORT STAIRS
AND ONTO THE ROOF.

JOHN JEREMY GAVE THEM
A CONFIDENT GLANCE.
"COME, UP TO THE ROOF.
IT'S OUR VERY LAST CHANCE!"

TEN MEN HELD A BLANKET AS TIGHT AS A DRUM. McGRUMP GAVE A SIGNAL THAT DOWN THEY SHOULD COME. THE BOY WAS THE FIRST, THEN THE SERVANTS, THE DAUGHTER, THEN EVERYONE WAITED FOR MRS. HYTHE-POTTER. SHE SAT ON THE ROOF, PALE AND FROZEN WITH FEAR. "I SIMPLY CAN'T DO IT," SHE SAID WITH A TEAR. "YOU MUST, MY DEAR LADY," JOHN JEREMY SAID. "JUST HOLD ON TO ME. THERE'S NOTHING TO DREAD." THE ROOF WAS NOW BURNING, ITS TIMBERS AGLOW. IT CRACKLED AND SPUTTERED AS IF TO SAY, "GO!" SO THEY CREPT TO THE EDGE AND LEAPT INTO THE AIR AND LANDED BELOW WITH MERE SECONDS TO SPARE.

For the house gave a groan and a gasp and a sigh, sparks flew in the air, lighting up the night sky. Then the rafters all buckled and fell to the ground. What a horrible sight! What a terrible sound!

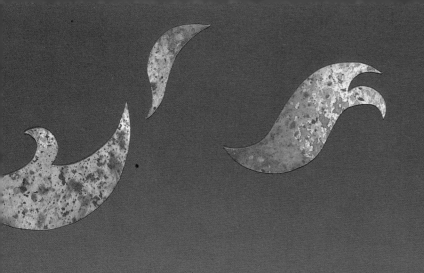

In the half-light that followed,

in the hour before day,

no one noticed

John Jeremy slipping away.

He went home to his house

and fell into bed,

for he ached and felt tired

from his toes to his head.

In the late afternoon

he awoke with a shock.

He heard music and voices

and a pounding

knock, knock!

He dressed in a minute

and opened the door.

And the moment he did so

he heard a great

ROAR. What a riotous cheer for John Jeremy Cotton was made by the folk in that village near Bolton! Everyone danced and a soloist sang. Firecrackers

and rockets went off with a bang.

Then Mrs Hythe-Potter said he was the best and what did it matter how anyone dressed? Heroes appear in the least likely places, and you can't tell who's brave by looking at faces.

Just where is that village, you're wanting to know? They say you can find it and the people who live there are the nicest you'll meet. Each house For if you're a stranger, they'll offer you tea, and a guest for a week will stay and a marvelous beauty that's hard to resist. It's down in a valley,

and easily so: rainbow-hued houses abound on each street,

...has a glory all of its own. You'll feel you belong there though far from your home.

...at least three. The town has an aura like sunlight through mist

...east that's what they say, a few miles from Bolton, up Lancashire way.

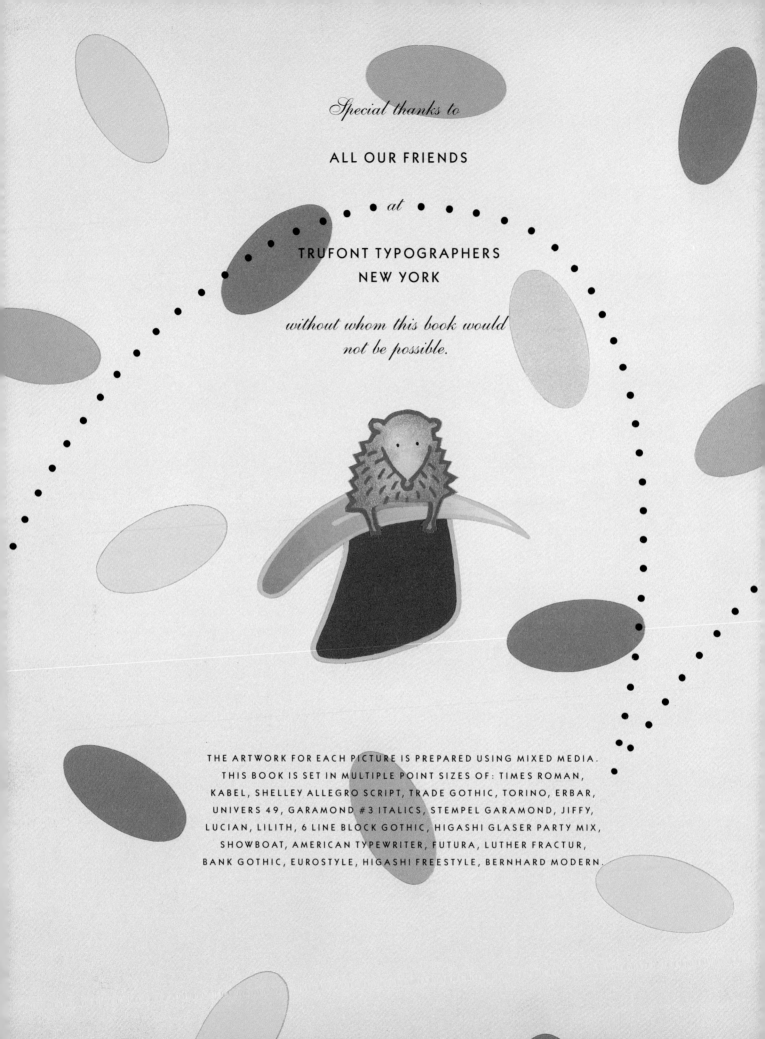

Special thanks to

ALL OUR FRIENDS

at

TRUFONT TYPOGRAPHERS
NEW YORK

*without whom this book would
not be possible.*

THE ARTWORK FOR EACH PICTURE IS PREPARED USING MIXED MEDIA.
THIS BOOK IS SET IN MULTIPLE POINT SIZES OF: TIMES ROMAN,
KABEL, SHELLEY ALLEGRO SCRIPT, TRADE GOTHIC, TORINO, ERBAR,
UNIVERS 49, GARAMOND #3 ITALICS, STEMPEL GARAMOND, JIFFY,
LUCIAN, LILITH, 6 LINE BLOCK GOTHIC, HIGASHI GLASER PARTY MIX,
SHOWBOAT, AMERICAN TYPEWRITER, FUTURA, LUTHER FRACTUR,
BANK GOTHIC, EUROSTYLE, HIGASHI FREESTYLE, BERNHARD MODERN.

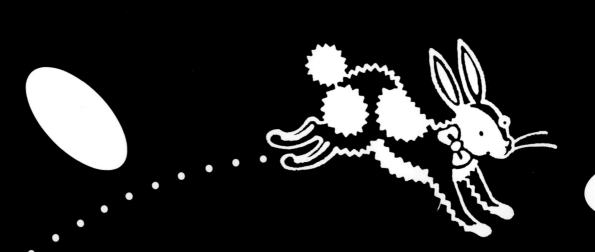

FIRST EDITION
1 3 5 7 9 10 8 6 4 2

LIBRARY OF CONGRESS CATALOGING-IN-PUBLICATION DATA

John Jeremy Colton / by Bryan Jeffery Leech : illustrated and
designed by Sandra Higashi & Byron Glaser - 1st ed.
p. cm.
Summary: Although shunned by his neighbors because of his oddly
colored house, John Jeremy Colton proves he is capable of being a
hero in a time of crisis.
ISBN 1-56282-650-6 (trade)   ISBN 1-56282-651-4 (lib. bdg.)
[1. Individuality - Fiction. 2. Fires - Fiction. 3. Stories in rhyme.]
I. Higashi, Sandra, ill. II. Glaser, Byron, ill. III. Title.

PZ8.3.L49935Jo   1994
[E] - dc20   93-2472
                                                  CIP
                                                  AC